Rushika J Hathi

(Author, Motivational Speaker, Corporate Trainer & Life Coach)

Make Your Life Ridiculously Amazing

Book*Squirrel* Publication

Make Your Life Ridiculously Amazing

Book*Squirrel* Publication

Regd. Under MSME Act.

"Make Your Life Ridiculously Amazing"

By: Rushika J. Hathi

ISBN: 978-93-89557-20-6

English

1st Edition

Editor: Bansi Chhatralia

Cover:Rushika Hathi & Team

Formatting; Mr_Ash

<u>Pouring the Heart and Dedication</u>

I am extremely grateful that this book is with you. You have chosen something very incredible, which will ease your life. It took me 2 years to complete the book and give you the nectar of my experience. This book will lead you to smile from the heart and you will feel that happiness is in your hands but you blame destiny and luck.

I dedicate this book to all of you and pray for "Making your Life Ridiculously Amazing". I would love to thank my family, mentors, friends, students, and the team who kept my spirit up while I complete this book. Let all of us be the support of each other in getting success. Begin now and feel the magic happening in your life.

CONTENTS

1. A HAPPY MANTRA --------------------05
2. REAL HAPPINESS: SMILE------------07
3. FOLLOW YOUR WORDS--------------11
4. CREATE YOUR OWN WORTH------14
5. YOU ARE YOUR OWN HERO--------17
6. PREPARE FOR THE WORST---------19
7. FAMILY SYNDROME-------------------22
8. JEALOUSY RUINS GROWTH---------25
9. HANDLE EMOTIONS-LEARN--------29
10. COMMIT TO STOP JUDGING
    PEOPLE----------------------------------30
11. LOVE & CARE IS THE REMEDY-
    GIVE!------------------------------------35
12. HEALTH IS FOREMOST--------------37
13. MOTIVATION VS INSPIRATION----41
14. ATTIRE IS ATTITUDE----------------44
15. MIND YOUR OWN BUSINESS-------46
16. CREATE NO SUBSTITUTE FOR
    YOURSELF-------------------------------49
17. WHAT IS A COST OF SMILE--------52
18. AUTHOR'S POCKET------------------53
19. EXPERT INTERVIEWS BY THE
    EDITOR----------------------------------54
20. ABOUT THE AUTHOR----------------69

1. A HAPPY MANTRA

If you are able to see it for yourself as a magician, then life is fully magical. All the tricks of happiness lie within you. The thing which needs to be changed is your thought process.

Happiness will be temporary if you let others be the source of your happiness. You are the only source who has to work for it to make it permanent. The very simple fact is **"You deserve to be happy; you deserve to live a life which you are excited about. Don't let others make you forget that."**

Happiness begins internally, therefore the first step would be to start loving yourself. When you start loving yourself automatically you start loving everything. We are here on the earth with the sole purpose to be happy & to make others happy.

This magical world offers us infinite beautiful things which we should experience instead of wasting our time on things which destroy us.

Happiness lies in many things i.e. happy faces of parents when we started walking for the first time, bunking our lectures for the first time, spending time with our loved ones, when we got to ride a car or scooter for the first time, admiring a newborn baby and many more like these. The list is endless.

So, here's to a dazzling you, Please look within yourself, love yourself, feel the madness of happiness. I know this would be a wonderful experience.

2. REAL HAPPINESS: SMILE

I want everyone to know that real happiness comes by smiling. We are missing the most beautiful thing that is a smile. Though it is free of cost, but it has incredible value.

On the basis of my understanding & experience, I can bet you that smile is the medicine that has the ability to cure dangerous diseases like anger, jealousy & ego.

But here we have to consider that it has some 'Not so good' effects too. It can create a fight also if used in a sarcastic way. It can be a catalyst for fights. Therefore, we need to use it wisely.

Everybody has a different and unique smile but it sends the same message. The biggest problem is that we need reasons to be happy &to smile. But a question here is why we need a reason to smile?

Let us give a smile to a stranger on road, a smile to a baby, a smile to that old woman who walks every day to the temple, etc.

Life is very short. If you don't smile today, then there is no tomorrow. Days will pass & struggles will increase. But a smile makes you relieved from the stress in life.

If you are thinking of having problems then having a problem is a universal problem. Come out of that comfort zone and feel the beauty of this amazing world.

Let us take the resolution "Not to be miser" in giving a smile. Let us open up in a beautiful way. I have seen many who feel like they don't look good while smiling or they are shy to smile in public, or they feel that they will look funny.

Few others don't smile back when I smile at them. Some avoid meeting people due to their silly reasons etc. But let us change our mind-sets a little so that we genuinely feel berated while smiling.

Every little smile can change somebody's heart. No one is born happy. But all of us are born with the ability to create happiness.

I can say that Smile has the ability to solve the most complicated issues in our life. Mostly 'relationship' it surely plays the role of unsaid words.

I would love to quote here, "Laughter begins with a smile" or I can say that "Laughter is the superlative degree of smile."

We must laugh every day. This sounds crazy but laughter actually changes our psychological state of mind and releases endorphins which are known as "Feel good chemicals." This actually has the potential to make people stress free and builds a strong immune system. It also can kill the pain of our stressful life.

We trust "Google Baba" more in today's world. It also says that after smiling the emotions which comes out are the overall feeling of happiness and calms the overall body.

In 2012, a study found out that laughter gives us pain tolerance hormones. So guys, if you are in pain due to any injury or illness watch funny movies or attend a comedy show.

If anybody like me who has a dream of living for 100 years on earth, then there is good news for all of us. A 2010 study shows that smiling is also associated with increased life spans.

Do not search for the happiness outside, it's within. It lies in the person you love the most, it lies in the broken teeth of old people, it lies everywhere. We need to search for it.

Just feel the miracle with every smile you give to others. I know this is silly but it is the only happiness found under your nose.

The only curve which we should be looking forward to is that curve on your face which is your smile. So let us decide that we will smile & spread happiness around us to create a positive atmosphere which would lead to a healthy lifestyle.

3. FOLLOW YOUR WORDS

In this world, we come across many people who are two-faced. Two-faced means their actions are totally different from what they say. This becomes totally contradictory.

Life is full of tragedies but we must have guts to convert these tragedies into positive energy. Whatever we speak must be our actions also. Because in this amazingly beautiful world, if we can't stick to our words, how are we going to make our nation proud.

We always complain about others regarding their manners, their inhumane nature, their words, their actions, etc. But have we ever seen what deep inside us regarding the same things? Perhaps No! Because we are always busy in judging others. Being harsh and rude is easy, but being simple & easy is really hard.

When we say-

"I am speaking the truth always." (Which we do occasionally now) Do we really see within ourselves that are we not lying many of the times?

"I have never hurt anyone and have never harmed society." Are we sure that we are not selfish? People know your actions.

"I always do social work and tell others about it." (Then please don't post in social media.)

"I never misuse power. I always follow my ethics." (Are we sure that we have not taken the seats of poor general caste person by paying 50000/-) Then we should know that we are not so ethical.

"I am always on time as I respect to time" (But when we were invited as a guest in some event, we have reached late by an hour because you are powerful & want people to wait for you.) Isn't it?

I never talk bad about people on their backs. How do other people do that? (And we are the one who were talking about a couple who got divorced due to genuine reasons in their lives)

There may be few things which might become harassment for someone, as you don't follow what you speak. And dual personality creates the worst circumstances at times. If you can't stick to your words, how can world? You influence the world. You must be an example in a positive way. I have read somewhere, "Follow your own words & your bliss and the universe will open door where there were only walls."

See for what you speak & follow your soul and your instinct.

4. CREATE YOUR OWN WORTH

The dictionary meaning of worth is usefulness or importance. It's like creating the value of own self. In this context, the value can be in terms of money which a person has or even a person who is an expert in this field, when nobody would doubt your teachings. Here we have to make sure not to harm anyone.

Because playing with anyone's emotions & feelings will lead to your downfall in life. After achieving great heights you will suddenly fall if you don't act wisely. And it would be very difficult to rise at this level once you fall due to your foolish actions. Therefore mind it before you get injured.

Mark Victor Hansen rightly said –

"When your self-worth goes up your net worth goes up with it."

Developing self-worth is really important. Analyse yourself and give time for self-improvement because we only have to make improvements in our self to create our worth in the crowd.

For the last 5 years, I am dealing with many people who want to have a big stage before working hard for it who wants instant money, fame who wants to become an idol for people out there. But I would like to say that firstly we need to work hard for this and be smart & not over smart in tackling the situation in life. Also taking calculated risks & making a win-win situation for all is beneficial.

It is possible to achieve what you want after all the hard work & labor you put into it. The world nowadays is creating win-lose scenarios and people think that others should fail.

Isn't it possible that we hold each other's hand & create a world without chaos by helping whenever we can? We can't improve or change other people but we surely can be the one who improves for a better world.

When you create your worth, the world will come to your feet. People will be inspired & motivated by you. Therefore I believe that we should be very pure and deal with things with transparency in order to avoid chaos

As there is no substitute for being extra good, achieve the level of goodness that your comparison would be impossible, as you inspire people to perform good deeds in life.

5. YOU ARE YOUR OWN HERO

We are so fond of certain people who are termed as heroes of society, due to their good deeds. We try to follow their way of living. We try to copy certain things from their lives i.e. how they speak, what they wear, what are their choices etc. We try & imitate the person as a whole.

But do we ever think the other way round? What if others observe us and follow us? What if we inspire people & become their hero?

It sounds very mesmerizing! What keeps me going is the process of being my own hero. This way I don't have to be dependent on others for my own happiness. You choose to be your own source of freedom. Real heroes are someone who seeks smile & happiness from others, which makes him/her a different person altogether. The love is as selfless & pure as the few drops which settle on the leaves after the rain. "Purity & transparency" are the two most precious things one can find in a hero.

You call them by any name. Whether it is a hero, idol, leader or superman, their first quality would be purity. He will be the one who will chase down the growth of himself and of others as well. He creates a win-win situation. As for us, it would be difficult some time to stay down to earth because our heads are filled with a disastrous device called Ego.

If we gain the stability of mind, have patience & understanding, we can earn fame and money. But before all of this, we have to become the most decent & selfless human being. These are my personal views because I can feel the magnificence of that bliss.

We are always searching for the person who can be our hero/idol. Rather why can't we 'Be the one'. We can be our own hero and in this journey of life, we can be an inspiration for others.

6. PREPARE FOR THE WORST

Life is like a storm. A storm that either destroys the entire farm or destroys the weeds and makes a place for growing the new crops. This means that we should always be ready for the worst consequences in life when we are on the way to "Make our like Ridiculously Amazing"

'Worst' is just word which scares us from the situation that is really awkward but as somebody rightly said **"This shall too pass"** So, here when the situation is worst the most important thing we need is the stability of mind. We mainly lack here because we are full of negativities and attached to this materialistic world.

How one can have time to interfere in the matters of others. Or why does one want to waste time in harassing or gossiping about someone?

Something we need to powder upon is on our thought process & our mind-sets. I believe that we should be prepared for anything & everything because in the end **"Everything happens for a good reason."**

A person must pass through all the filters in life and make it more amazing. Filters in terms of loyalty, truth, honesty, kindness, friendship, love, etc. These are some tests in life which we need to pass. The passing of these tests includes many unwanted things which make us confident in life. i.e. - the outcome of these tests might be inclusive of struggle, insults, mood swings, anger, etc. But it will lead us to a beautiful life experience too.

Preparing for the worst is like being ready to fight the war with our own selves sometimes. And it could be fearful times. For example, in a job, you are following the path of truth & obedience and you even don't like corruption. But this way some people won't support you and in the end, you are fired from the job.

This could be a depression period for you or maybe a fight with your own self, but you can frame this experience of yours as a struggle story of your life.

Another instance of you being in a relationship and you say whatever you feel and it may lead to a fight sometimes due to difference in opinions & mindsets of two people in a relationship. But this could be manageable if your relationship is strong and true then it won't break.

Give your best efforts into it and even if it breaks then don't regret it, it's your destiny that gives you the experience to learn from. You would be stronger to face the situation than ever before if you act wisely.

Trust yourself, your deeds, your inner voice & your genuine efforts too. Worst can be anything that will mould you into a better human being. Because life is all about celebrating smaller & larger moments and not regretting what has already happened in the past which can't be altered.

7. FAMILY SYNDROME

Family is the first place where values are built. It can mould a person in many ways. It can make or break the person entirely. So, the family plays a very vital role.

It makes the life of a person if there is great support from them. But contradictory things, conservations and rigid culture may ruin the life of a person. This chapter is dedicated to parents & to be parents.

I would love to quote here that **"Every child is important and let us value each of them."**

We are living in modern society and this world is going to be super-fast in the future. We as a parent must see that our kids can survive in this cruel world. We need them to be a power pack combo of everything in terms of education, patience, household work, job/business, a perfect personality, convincing nature, humility and everything which would make them stable in life.

But sometimes we stop them from being best, we judge them and taunt them on the basis of our experiences. Yes, we are emotional and we have many expectations from them and would want them to reach great heights. We want them to do whatever we desired but we are not able to complete them due to circumstances & the situations, which were extremely different in our times.

Bhagwad Gita also says- **"If you want the real growth of your child, let them experience by themselves. Don't give them everything without any effort."**

There are many parents who have been torturing their children and ask them to follow their orders, i.e. there are cases when a child is forced to choose a career option which he/she dislikes. The child is forced for getting married early etc. And parents want them to do whatever they say.

Our children are our souls and let them be free. We must trust their ability and values.

Here, I want to use the word Please, as I have seen children craving for 'Love' from their parents. Please, it's an urge to respected parents, let this seed grow and become a tree in their own beautiful way. So, it can give shed and fruits to society.

Nurture them with proper understanding, love, values, ethics and little freedom for their growth.

Note to children: Do not misuse the freedom given to you because you don't know how parents are killing their dreams just to complete yours.

8. JEALOUSY RUINS GROWTH

The biggest disaster in the world is jealousy. It creates misunderstanding & complications too. This is because when we are jealous, we spread negativity & negative vibes will run around in our body and mind. We won't be able to think good about others because I truly believe that what we think, we start becoming the one.

When we are jealous of someone or in fear of losing our so-called name & fame, we start doing the wrong things, we trust rumors easily & also try to betray people in ways we can.

When we start focusing on bad things of others, we can't see good in them. By doing so we are just wasting our precious time and start making someone feel divested. We are compromising our greatness to prove someone's mediocrity.

In this world full of people believing in comparisons regarding the materialistic things, they are forgetting their own calibre and strengths. They are evaporating their power by not focusing on actual things in life.

People will be blessed if they help and they are kind to others. When we support others in their need but we tend to forget the selflessness and we become selfish, spread negative vibes instead of powerful ones around us. The people who are suffered by us will curse us and this cycle is endless if we don't act wisely.

Therefore, let's pledge that we would avoid the jealousy factor which makes us selfish, and would try to spread the fragrance of love & kindness. As it is rightly said, **"What we give we will surely receive, as the earth is round."**

Let us always try to cultivate the habit of being the winner or champion by helping people around us. Let us avoid measuring our powers & fame. People will judge you on the basis of what you speak. Hence it will lead to the stoppage of your own development & happiness.

So, let us be blissful & spread happiness so in return we will be gifted by the true smile given by others because of the inner joy & satisfaction.

9. HANDLE EMOTIONS-LEARN

Emotions- Yes, an aspect that plays a significant role in everyone's life. **But we fail to manage them.** Therefore we commit a huge mistake by giving reactions to the actions in the wrong way.

The biggest thing that we lack is our stability of mind. We have a habit of showing our emotions in one or the other way. But this cruel world is not ready to accept the real emotions. They will play with the same and we would get hurt. I usually come across complaints when a person is hurt. One feels that people are cruel and unable to understand their feelings. But I believe that the real scenario is we are dependent on somebody for our happiness and moods. **We must develop our self in such a way that we are able to manage our own emotions.**

An emotion in our life is one of the temporary phases which is not permanent. But we have a habit of overthinking on each and every emotion of ourselves. And we are responsible for drowning ourselves into the sea of sadness.

We have to train our mind to be stronger and stable to handle our emotions or else we will lose our self every time. **If we are willing to control everything, firstly we have to control our thoughts and then emotions.** We are searching for peace in material things. We look forward to our holidays for relaxing and to gain peace of mind and are dependent on others for many things. I believe that we are a bit wrong here. Peace lies in our minds and heart.

Sem Brown has quoted in this regard- **"You must be master of your emotions if you wish to live in peace, for he who can control himself becomes free."** We always try to control what is going around us and we forgot to look within ourselves. Hence, we fail in controlling traffic.

Wayne Dyer said – **"You cannot always control what goes on outside. But you can always control what's going inside."**

The core need for our survival is money. But due to our poor behaviour and uncontrollable emotions, we lose money too.

While closing even any business deal we must have patience and ice on the head.

Once Warren Buffet tweeted- **"You will continue to suffer if you have an emotional reaction to everything that is said to you. True power is sitting back and observing things with logic. True power is restraint. If words control you that means everyone can control you. Breathe and allow things to pass."**

He further said, **"If you cannot control your emotions, you cannot control your money."**

Whenever and whatever the circumstances occur a scenario of either **"Fight or Flight",** that means if there is any emotional imbalance, **we either can become stable and fight or we become coward and flight(run).** We need to be dependent on ourself solely for the happiness we deserve. We should have faith in our skills and abilities. It would make us into a fantastic emotional manager of our life.

10. COMMIT TO STOP JUDGING PEOPLE

We all love doing one thing that is "Judging others" when we are casually sitting free we start analysing people based on our thought process and we judge.

We frame very weird opinions about others and we confidently spatter out to the world. Even we are not sure whether it is true or false. Because it is based on the circumstances occurring around or how the person behaving with us?

Who has given us the right of framing a dreadful judgment about others? While being judgemental we feel we are doing something great on the basis of our thinking pattern but yes, it also reveals our personality. It might be good or cheap depends on the judgment we passed.

From the opinions that we framed, they are giving birth to the injurious virus & that is "Gossip". Gossip and rumours go hand in hand. It spreads like a wind fire.

I believe that we should stop all this as we never know someday we might end up being in the same worst situation. Few instance framing opinions are listed below-

"She is fat and not doing exercises, very irresponsible." But we don't see that "She" is a thyroid patient and is in pain.

"Oh! At the age of 33 years, he is not married and not earning anything." (Do we know that he is in depression as his father died before 5 years and mother is a cancer patient?)

"Look she is happy, she is having lots of money and she doesn't have any problem. We are unlucky. She can buy 50 pairs of clothes for an entire week. (Do we know that "she" is adopted a child and being harassed by her step-parents? So, she goes to the orphanage and distributes those clothes to kids there.)

"She is such a useless person and has the less mental capacity to understand things. She always laughs and smiles at little things. (That "She" is beaten each day due to poor family culture and rigid mentality.

So, she has decided to make everyone happy with her smile.)

"These are stupid & nonsense people who are in love with each other. How can they be such idiots?" (They might have loved the soul of each other and promised to take care of both the families. In this owed world they might have actually found someone very true & loyal by heart.)

"Their daughter is having a physical problem, she is almost 31 years old. She won't get a good groom. One must get settled at the age of 23 years." (Hello "that daughter" has physical problems by birth, not her fault. See the inner beauty; she has made someone's life more beautiful. We are always ready for backbiting, if she would be your daughter then?)

"She might have done something nonsense that's why she is beaten and threaten even she is forced to marriage."("She" is the most innocent girl loving and respecting parents but due to rigid mentality and power, she is the prey. She cares so she is not taking the legal actions.)

"She is so busy that she never answers call." ("She" might be solving somebody's missed puzzle and she is not free for gossip. Message her. The call is not the only solution.)

"She never pays money, each time I pay. She must have that courtesy." ("She" is craving for one time meal because she has no money for bread & butter.)

"She speaks less and she is a kind of an introvert." ("She" has faced insult when she spoke the truth in public and she is going through a bad phase. She hates backbiting and bitching. She loves the development of people done silently by her.)

We are not wearing someone's shoes and therefore we don't know what it is costing the other person who is actually going through some difficulty.

So, let us stop judging people and try to know the actual reason behind any action before we take a final decision, as we don't know the other side. Even I have seen people who judge randomly other's opinion. But we must use our brain and heart as melody is perfect.

I will love to quote here that "Those who spend their time looking for faults in others, usually spend no time to correct their own."

Let us not judge people by what they follow and believe in life. Because we never know what are they going through. Let us throw kindness around like confetti. We can be a little less judgmental about things that are going around us (Especially in others' life) to make our life more peaceful & beautiful.

11. LOVE & CARE IS THE REMEDY-GIVE!

We are extremely happy when we receive love and feel happiness. But at times we feel really stressed that we end up in the wrong impression that "Nobody loves me." This is because we are soaking ourselves in the ocean of expectations and desires.

We find ourselves in a situation where there is no way to get out of it, we try to harm ourselves also. Due to this, we spoil our mental & physical health.

The secret behind everybody's need is receiving an abundance of love, care & respect. It has a magical power to heal and calm each living being. Care is the default part of a beautiful thing called "Love".

In brief, I can pen down is, "Loving someone is not only the emotions as it is more about thoughts. Thinking and making the person happy who we love the most. Well caring for the person just as much as you care for yourself that's what I feel love is."

I titled this chapter as-"Love & care is the remedy- Give", just because if we give love we are more contented than receiving it because there is no scope of any expectation here. There is abundance of understanding and giving always.

There is a mystery behind giving love and care. When you give love to someone it can heal the health of person. Love renews and restores the inner self because each cell in our body is harmonious to this natural healing state.

Healing starts the moment you align your mental and emotional frequency which collides with love.

"Love is care, love is power, and love is the magic of changes,

Love is the mirror of divine beauty."

-

Rumi

We are always stuck with fear or anxiety. By this, we are disconnecting ourselves from wisdom. This leads to the creation of inaccurate mental stage expressed in the body as illness.

Dr. David Hawkins affirms: "Choosing to become a loving person results in the release of endorphins by the brain which has a profound effect on the body's health and happiness."

Care and love are the main ingredients in the delicious recipe called life. When we become a giver instead of taker it can become a remedy for all the problems. We make a living by what we get, but we make a life by what we give.

Giving is the highest expression of our power. I would request that,

"There is nothing wrong with being a little more giving in life. After all, there has to be someone who gives light in a darkened room." Ruy Dhal

12. HEALTH IS THE FOREMOST

When we have money, we can have power, people, family, material things, etc. **But if not good health, then we won't be able to enjoy all these things in life.** Irrespective of having everything in life, we are not able to live it to the fullest due to our poor health. Therefore we should make health our priority. We have a tradition of saying that **"We don't have time for us."** And if we are really busy with other things, we are surely going to lose our top mate- **'Health'.**

Always invest in self-care for future gains. When we take care of ourselves, we can be a better being in terms of being a friend, a partner, a spouse or a parent. We would be able to take care of others if we ourselves are in a good state (physically and mentally).

When we are fit we will be more energetic and confident in performing our everyday tasks. But when we are not focusing on our health we are going to feel hassle over everything and we would start overthinking. These monsters are really dangerous for our intellectual strength. And when we are not emotionally strong, we are going to lose physical health for sure. If physical health is deteriorated than we can suffer from tiredness and laziness. We are not in a mood to talk, with people and because of all these things we might lose relationships or we might miss an important day in office.

At this point we should improve our quality of sleep, should develop our eating habits, and should also ensure that we exercise or meditate. All these things would nurture our body and will allow us to live a better life.

We need to make some efforts and develop some good habits in order to ensure that we would be physically fit in order to live a healthy lifestyle. **The best thing about taking care of ourselves is we will radiate glow from inside and skin will be full of vitality, this is because Collagen(the main structural protein found in skin and other connective tissues, widely used in purified form for cosmetic surgical treatments)is produced.** When we invest in our health we will get interest in many forms i.e. in the form of some money which won't be spent on medicines. Our medical bills could be reduced by this.

The most Confident Personality would have awesome physical health. If we are fit then surely we will be mentally stable in life and if we properly care about our health, with the help of proper nutrition and addition of exercise to it than it does wonder. We will be more enthused to take any challenge personally or professionally.

Let us commit now to ourselves that health will be our topmost priority. We will make ourselves fit and healthy in order to live a better life. And also will help people who are not fit (mentally and physically).

While doing all these things in life, we maintain our good health and become the best edition of ourselves. And can enjoy this amazing life ridiculously.

13. MOTIVATION VS INSPIRATION

Motivation refers to a "force or influence that causes someone to do something." People these days are craving for motivation here and there. They want someone to boost them up every minute. They also want someone to be by their side 24/7 and protect them or motivate them in ways they expect. But I feel that why do we need this? **There is only one person who can motivate us and that person is really astonishing and of course, that is "YOU"**. Nobody knows us more than ourselves. We sometimes devalue our self and get demotivated. And we seek motivation from outer source.

We will be motivated for a certain period of time when we hear any motivational speech or attend any motivational seminar or hear our friends consoling words. **But when we are, inspired by someone then we could be for a lifetime or for the time period till we become what we want to. Inspiration from anything or anyone awakens us to new possibilities by allowing us to transcend ourselves. A peg of inspiration mixed with some dedication**

in life can decide our journey from depressed to a successful life. As inspiration is a sharp weapon which can be used in tough times. It teaches us how to move smoothly in life on the roads which are bumpy. It may lead us to discover something new or do something beyond belief by keeping all our problems and worry aside.

As per my practice, we sometimes are so depressed in our life that we ignore our future by living in past memories. Here, inspiration gives us the feeling of positivity and diverts us to the elevation of success. **Like natural scenery is considered as beauty of the planet earth, inspiration is considered as the beauty of life. I can rather say inspiration is the rainbow of our life when the dark clouds surround us.**

According to an IBM survey of 1700 CEO's through 64 countries, the three leadership traits which are important are:

1. The ability to focus intensely on customer needs.
2. The ability to collaborate with colleagues, and

3. The ability to inspire.

Simon Sinek told us in his TED Talk, "How Great Leaders Inspire Action", No one follows a leader for the leader. They follow a leader for their attitude & personality. **The most inspirational leaders ignite a spark within their employees or followers which could move them in life. They don't require motivation to act because they have been inspired.**

In this era of rapid growth & development, we have to prove our self. We have to face everyone; we have to be the true version of our self without quitting. We will certainly need some time but slowly & gradually everything would fall into place. Therefore let us attempt and be the inspiration to others and inspire more to achieve goals. **No matter whatever struggles we come across, we should be stimulated from the heart and then nobody can stop us from winning the world or to accomplish our dreams.**

14. ATTIRE IS ATTITUDE

"Enclothed Cognition" is research that signifies that the clothes which we wear affect our confidence, personality, attitude, and mood and also the way we interact with people. For instance are we feeling sad, upset or weird? Then let us change what we are wearing. It will at least give us a sense of relief.

Our intellectual state also affects the way we dress. The apparels we wear could affect us in certain ways **i.e. when we are tensed, depressed or worried. Research states that we can light up our mood when we wear bright colours clothes. Bright colours make us feel energetic and we can cheer ourselves up.** For example when we are in professional attire, we feel so confident about ourselves, like we are ready to conquer the world.

When we meet/see a person for the first time we try to figure out the personality on the basis of the clothes he/she is wearing. It never matters from where the clothes have been purchased i.e. are they branded or purchased from the street market. The selection of clothes is the only thing which matters the most.

I would like to draw your attention here that why should we look beautiful and attractive only on special occasions? **Rather we should be bold, stunning and act smart every day. As every one of us is beautiful inside out. Let us dress ourselves in such a way that no one can bend our confidence level.**

Trust me; there are few people around us, who will start praising our work and responsibilities just by observing our dressing sense. If you act smart and dress prudently you can be an icon or an inspiration to others. Our attire is our attitude and it could also reveal our emotions at times. Therefore, we must think at least once, whenever we dress up for an occasion.

Let us make our life perfectly amazing by wearing our attitude positively in the form of our attire.

15. MIND YOUR OWN BUSINESS

Life is full of struggle and trouble. **A study shows that 55% of these are caused by our reaction. The reaction is still fine but what we do is interfere in other's matters even when they don't ask. We are least concerned about ourselves and our work.**

-We enjoy peeping into other's life more. We become the best advisors when others are in a problem. I think that what happens with us when it is our case?

- We all are experts in passing judgment when somebody tells us something about others. We do have a habit of judging people on basis of any random things/events. And when others judge us or talk about us we feel extremely bad and do anything to prove ourselves right.

- We are literally happy for interfering in someone's life without knowing the actuality in detail. We interfere and proceed with our thought process and want others to act according to our will. By doing this we feel that we are an inspiration to them. But the case is not so. It might have a reverse effect on another person.

- Even we try and dominate people with our power and misuse it too. We feel really powerful if we can terrorize someone or physically harass them. What I believe is KARMA has its own ways and what we do will surely come to us someday.

And what we forget is that the almighty up there is always watching us. We become helpless when we are endangered or physically harassed by a person. Here we try to look out for someone who can support or save us. Then why do we have a custom of troubling others?

Why do we forget to mind our business? Why are we being so selfish? Why are we so rude? Aren't we supposed to stop this nonsense and keep the pace alive?

I have a humble request to all the beings out there. Let us all make this world a beautiful place to live in. Let us help and support each other in ways we can. Also, can we change our age-old mentality about certain things? Yes, peace of mind and good things are in our

hands. We should spread our love and should mind our own business. We have to respect everybody's thoughts.

16. CREATE NO SUBSTITUTE FOR YOURSELF

The dictionary meaning of substitute is "a person or thing that takes the place of someone or something else." But when we do not find the one we are confused and disappointed about why are we unsuccessful in finding the substitute of the original one.

In this context, it signifies that we should be the limited edition of ourselves because if our substitute is found then our value will be decreased, as people will look out for somebody more interesting than us. **Let us be unique, do something very surprising, let us be an expert in our field and I bet nobody can beat us.** I believe that we are fearless and can build a strong personality. For this, we must educate ourselves first try and experiment on different aspects, take calculative risks and try doing creative things in life. Let us make our self so outstanding that people will look only for US. **Because nobody can steal our knowledge, nature, and expertise.**

Stop following the advice which makes us feel, that this does not make sense to us.

Because what we are going through will not be the same situation through which the adviser is going. He/she might not have the same problems as ours.

Be the branded version of yourself because the first copy is just a craze but a branded piece has its own worth. When our thinking and vision are bigger we will be able to do anything but we do fear people. Therefore in my view I think that with vision and thinking our risk-taking ability and courage should also be bigger. Let us introspect our thoughts and start loving our self. Doors of something very amazing will open by itself.

The problem lies in comparing ourselves with others. We have to leave aside this comparing strategy in order to develop ourselves in a constructive way.

"Be someone with whom no competition can be done."

We usually become upset when somebody copies our style, strategies, and thoughts. But this is an excellent sign as we have done something very well which

others have no idea of and they attempt to copy us.

The moral of the story is to stop complaining and demanding. Just be the greatest copy of yourself and do something extra beautiful which nobody has ever thought of. Change the mindset and the way of thinking. Commit to create our own monopoly in such a way that nobody could have our substitute.

And always remember there is only one Mother Teresa, only one Mahatma Gandhi, Only one Hitler, only one Narendra Modi, only one Shobha Bhutada, only one P V Sindhu and the list goes on. And there has to be only ONE YOU. Be the one and make things wonderful.

Make Your Life Ridiculously Amazing

What is the cost of a smile?

Take a sneak peek to the story of - The Chef and The Gatekeeper

The story is all about a very famous hotel. The chef had one good quality. He would always greet everyone with a 'smile' irrespective of whether a person is known or unknown to him and irrespective of what post a person is in. One the other hand the gatekeeper was reactionless.

Whenever the chef used to arrive or depart he would greet the gatekeeper with a smile but would get nothing in return. The same thing continued for months.

One day as ill fate would have it, the hotel was on the verge of closing. But the gatekeeper didn't see the chef coming out of the hotel. He then tried to recall whether he came the same morning or not.

To which he found that the chef arrived at the hotel. Out of curiosity the gatekeeper entered the hotel and started searching for him. After a 10 minutes interrogation and searching the gatekeeper was left without any clue. But he thought to give one final try.

When he entered the store area he found that the chef was lying there unconscious.

Without wasting more time the gatekeeper called the ambulance and accompanied him to the hospital where it was found that the chef had suffered a massive cardiac arrest.

This brings us to a very small but important question. What if the chef would have stopped greeting the gatekeeper??

Would he be alive today???

Definitely not...

And it also brings us to the most important conclusion as well as the best answer to people who ask that What is the cost of a smile and Why smiling is important because sometimes a smile can save your life too...

FROM AUTHOR'S POCKET

Life is the melodious song- Sing it

Life is the Act of kindness- Give it

Life is the feeling of success- Celebrate it

Life is the madness with love- Feel it

Life is the amazing journey- Live it

Together we have to

"Make our Life Ridiculously Amazing"

#TrustandbelieveinYourself

Expert Interviews by Editor

-Bansi Chhatralia//-

SHOBHA BHUTADA
(Director, Intelligence
Bureau, DELHI, INDIA)

1. Rushika believes in "Making Life Ridiculously Amazing" and living it fully. Do you believe in this?

Yes! I strongly believe in Rushika's Life Mantra. She is such a strong positive believer and making other's life amazing by spreading kindness to society.

I do follow her statement that your life is magic and there is only one life. Live it fully, where you face happiness, love, and sorrow-all at one!

Make your routine amazing, your thoughts; your lifestyle is what makes you amazing.

These are just noted points but the main thing is that "You" Yourself is the Creator of Your Deeds. So Do Good Be Good That's it and then Strong belief towards your good deeds will lead you to the goal of your life!

Explore yourself to the Love and Kindness vibes from the Universe will make it's happening.

2. What would you like people to remember about you and your Profession?

Being a part of Cop I am very much glad and proud of myself that I'm serving my country. I am proud Indian and I Respect My Profession. For Me My Profession is everything.

I serve society, fight for right, and protect the country. For me this duty and this designation is everything.
I am working for years and now imp fully involved with my work. Being Fierce is my passion.
My work speaks out everything.

3. Share your views about Rushika Hathi as a Person.

Rushika Hathi!
One of my favorite bloggers and after knowing her better I became her 'Fan-based' Friend and Guide, though I didn't meet her personally. But I must say she is doing her best for the society and her knowledge relate to the content and her blogs are Amazing, the content she creates through her magical words is just Wow! At very young age she is encouraging Youth and training people is great. That's what I admire about her work every time. Being a part of the TEDx speaker list is also an achievement for her. She is a positive personality and doing best for society. I wish her lots of success and support with blessings for her making her every dream come true! Padma Bhushan is waiting for you. Lots of luck Rushika!
JAI HIND

BHAVIN SHAH
(Motivational Speaker |
Author | Corporate Trainer &
Mentor)

1. Rushika believes in "Making Life Ridiculously Amazing" and living it fully. Do you believe in this?

So, as you know, from day 1, I always say that one can only Make Life Ridiculously Amazing when one wants to live it. We see many people who don't want anything from their lives and they don't have that hunger. But I have also seen such people who want to grow their lives, who want to take their lives to a new level. So definitely, this should be the purpose of your life that how you can make your Life Ridiculously Amazing. One should be able to inspire others through. Now see, I don't think to make life ridiculously amazing is for one's personal life. If your life is ridiculously amazing, hundreds of thousands of people get inspired and make their own lives ridiculously amazing. Your family gets inspired by your life, they feel proud. Your community feels proud, your country feels proud. Making Life Ridiculously Amazing may seem like it is limited to oneself, but it is not that way. Making one life ridiculously amazing inspires other people to achieve what they want. So it is must to make your Life Ridiculously Amazing.

2. What would you like people to remember about you and your Profession?

The first thing I focus on our profession is working with the right intention. You have been in this profession for a long time now and you know that the only people who survive in this profession are the ones who are honest, work ethically and with values and whose intentions are good. You would have learned that in our profession, the part of ethics, etiquette, and intentions must be consistent. If you're doing it, do it consistently. The most important thing of all is Determination to solve any problem, any challenge. Grow with the team. Do not grow alone. That is very important. So these four parameters are I believe to learn from our profession.

3. Share your views about Rushika Hathi as a Person.

Rushika as a person is very optimistic, very positive. If you ask me, Rushika is the kind of person who can bring out water even from the desert. Where people start to lose hope is where Rushika's hope begins. She is the person who always focuses on the solution part of everything, believing in any case that "It will be done". That is what I love about Rushika that she always looks at things from a solution orientation. She is a result-oriented person. That's why many people have been inspired by her and a lot of women-empowerment has come through her. Holding to a small center like Porbandar and creating such an empire over there would have been possible for anyone else except Rushika. Rushika Hathi is the **Gabbar of Training Industries,** a name given by IMPOSSIBLE TRAINING INSTITUTE, Vadodara.

SUMIT ACHARYA

(In-charge Director, Shree
Swami Narayan Institute of
Management, Porbandar)

1. Rushika believes in "Making Life Ridiculously Amazing" and living it fully. Do you believe in this?

Yes, I do. I don't know whether you believe in next birth or not, but I do not. We just have one life and we are living it right now. So why not make it so large that it may become inspiration to at least a few people? Working for 7 days a week, 12 hours a day, coming back home, making dinner and going to sleep. Is it the routine of a human being? Are we sent on Earth just to earn our livelihood and leaving nothing behind? No… Human life is meant for many things. One has to spare time to make it purposeful. Try to complete your wishes. Let the world know about your dreams and the way you achieve them. A society where you live is also expecting your contribution. Spread some virtues in society to make the nation more powerful. Your all-cause should give you happiness and satisfaction from within. A happy heart can create many miracles. Living with a broad smile and joyful nature is the key success of human life.

2. What would you like people to remember about you and your Profession?

"Gurudev" is the word assigned to a teacher. The word itself clarifies its importance to be a path maker. A teacher by profession is a matter of chance, but satisfactorily completing and justifying this role is the biggest challenge and carries a lot of responsibilities. As I am a teacher by profession, the society has put up a lot of responsibilities on my shoulders. A child is handed over to a teacher with the hope to nurture him and making the best person who can lead the society… So the first duty of the teacher is to make himself capable enough so that the parents can keep a trust o him about wellness of their child. Being a teacher, we can observe varieties of students in a class and our responsibilities include to bring them to an equal platform and nurturing them so that they can become better citizens. I am thankful to God for considering me capable enough to serve society by educating the students about right path of their lives. I don't know whether I have succeeded or not in this profession, but yes, at least I am giving my best to them and I am happy about that.

3. Share your views about Rushika Hathi as a Person.

It's been almost 10 years since I have known Rushika Hathi. A very mature, humble and kind person. Yes, since day one when we came across during an academic session, she has shown a spark in her. Being a human being, she knows perfectly what she has to do. I know her in many roles when she is a daughter; she has always made her parents proud. As a student also, she has achieved stars in her grade sheets. As a friend she has always kept her promises and has never left anyone alone. But all in all, as a person she is a divine soul. When it comes to personal motive of her life, I can see that she lives for the society. She always initiates the things which help the society by putting her best efforts. It is very rare to find a person who thinks less about self and more about others. Yes, in a few words, I can define her as **"Divine Soul with Modern Appearance"**.

NAROTTAM PALAN

(Knowledgeable and learned Author)

1. Rushika believes in "Making Life Ridiculously Amazing" and living it fully. Do you believe in this?

The mantra is right that we should live our life amazingly. But we have to live in such a way that we should not harm anybody. We have to follow the ethics and we have to live in a way that we become 100% selfless. Serve the people and make their life amazing too.

2. What would you like people to remember about you and your Profession?

When I was in the 10th standard, I started writing and at that time my 3 books were published. Writing is my passion and we must never give up on our passion. This will make us feel alive. I have written many books and they are helpful to people for centuries.

3. Share your views about Rushika Hathi as a Person.

Rushika at a very young age is doing great for the society and helping many. Her women empowerment has led to a great height. She is doing great things for her own city Porbandar is a big asset. Salute to her and all the best.

About the Author

Rushika, a name among the common public was looking for self-development and society's growth. She is from simple background having **trained participants on Career Guidance, Interview Tactics, Personality Development, Recruitments, Parenting, Creativity in Teaching, Stress Management, Public Speaking, Sales Secrets, How to promote yourself?, Success Steps, Communication, and Presentation Skills, Employability Skills, Dealing with Exam fear, etc.**

Her mission is to bring out the hidden potential to have a bright future and the flowery journey ahead. She has trained 40000 plus participants.

A girl started her journey with Chartered Accountancy course came to Ahmedabad from Porbandar, failed 7 times and she has to quit the same. But interest level in dealing with people, she started with Masters in Human Resource Management. She worked with recruitment consultancy and started training recruiters, students, conducting seminars, workshops, etc. She wanted to create awareness in oneself. **Now she is successful Motivational Speaker, Life Coach & Corporate Trainer.** Apart from being a trainer, she is into writing blogs & articles.

Rushika is working in 7 cities of Gujarat as of now and wants to explore the world.

Services

- **Motivational Seminars and Workshops**
- **Corporate Trainings**
- **Trainings for schools and colleges**
- **Personal Coaching and Mentoring**

You can connect to Rushika at-

E-mail: rushikahathi@gmail.com

Number: 8160522737

Benefited Clients

- Dash Technologies @Ahmedabad

- Hotel Ramada, @Ahmedabad

- ITI, Upleta

- Yagyavalkya School, Porbandar

- Jetking, Porbandar

- Dalal Merchandise Advisory Private Limited, Visnagar

- Lions club of Porbandar

- Suruchi English Medium School Porbandar

- Parishram Job Placement and Computers, Porbandar

- Government Polytechnic College,Porbandar

- Shri Kasturba Mahila Mandal

- Gurukul Mahila College, Porbandar

- Lokmanya B.Ed College, Ahmedabad

- Swaminarayan School, Porbandar

- Brain Child Learning (Aloha), Ahmedabad

- Rotary Club, Porbandar

- INIFD

- Innerwheel Club, Porbandar

- District Chamber of Commerce, Porbandar

- Center for Entrepreneurship Development, Porbandar

- SnapSeaarch Consultants, Ahmedabad

- Vision Spring Solutions, Ahmedabad

- GLS college, Ahmedabad

- DDIT, Nadiad

- Skill Up gradation Center, Porbandar and many more.